Mog and the Granny

Judith Kerr

PictureLions

An Imprint of HarperCollinsPublishers

For Eve and Thomas
and their Granny and Grandpa

Have you read all these books by Judith Kerr?

Board Books

Mog's Family of Cats   Mog in the Garden
Mog and Me   Mog's Kittens

Picture Books

Mog the Forgetful Cat   Mog on Fox Night
Mog's Christmas   Mog and the Vee Ee Tee
Mog and the Baby   Mog's Amazing Birthday Caper
Mog and Barnaby   When Willy Went to the Wedding
Mog in the Dark   The Tiger Who Came to Tea
Mog and Bunny   How Mrs Monkey Missed the Ark

First published in Picture Lions in 1996 3 5 7 9 10 8 6 4 First published in Great Britain
by HarperCollins Publishers Ltd in 1995. Text and illustrations copyright © Judith Kerr 1995.
The author/illustrator asserts the moral right to be identified as the author/illustrator of the work.
A CIP catalogue for this title is available from the British Library. ISBN: 0 00 664592 5

One day Mog was waiting for Debbie
to come home from school.
Mog always knew when Debbie was coming.
She didn't know how she knew. She just knew.
Suddenly a picture would come into her head
of Debbie coming down the road.
Then she would go to meet her.
Debbie said, "School's all finished for
the summer, Mog. Isn't it exciting!"
Mog said nothing. She didn't like things
to be exciting. She liked them to be the same.

Inside the house
everyone was excited too.
Mrs Thomas was packing.

Mr Thomas
was looking
for something
important.

Nicky was dancing
and singing a song
he had made up.

"*We're going to America where the skyscrapers are.*
We're not going by train but on an aeroplane.
We'll see all the sights,
and it will be very
surprising because
they have their
days when we
have our
nights!"

Debbie said, "You can't come, Mog.
But you're going to a nice granny's house.
She'll look after you till we come back."

Next day Mog went to the granny's house.

The granny was old with very thin legs.

First Mog thought she had three legs.

Then she saw that one of them was a stick.

Debbie said, "Goodbye, dear Mog."

The granny said, "I'll look after Mog.

And she'll have my Tibbles for company."

Mog thought, "Tibbles? Nobody told me

that there would be another cat.

At least he sounds quite small."

Tibbles had been small to start with but then he had grown. "Here's a little friend for you," said the granny.

Tibbles liked surprising people.

And he liked Mog's basket. The granny said, "Don't be silly, Tibbles. Let Mog have her basket, and you can sleep on my bed."

Mog sat in her basket, but she couldn't sleep.
She thought of her house. She thought of Debbie.
Suddenly a picture of Debbie came into her head.
Debbie was in a high place and there were even
higher places all round. It was all too high.
Mog didn't think Debbie should be there.

"Whatever is the matter, Mog?" said the granny.

"You'd better come and snuggle up with us."

A few days later the postman brought a card.

"It's from Debbie," said the granny.

"She's been to the top of a skyscraper."

Mog thought the card smelled of Debbie.

Tibbles didn't have a card.

He had tea in a saucer instead.

He was very fond of tea.

Tibbles had an open window instead of a cat flap.
He had a yard to play in.

Sometimes Mog and Tibbles played together.

Sometimes they chased each other.

Sometimes they liked each other

and sometimes they didn't.

The granny gave them nice food to eat.
She went to the shops to buy it.
They always had the same, but they
always thought the other one's was nicer.

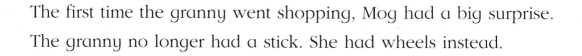

The first time the granny went shopping, Mog had a big surprise.
The granny no longer had a stick. She had wheels instead.

She gave Tibbles a ride.

"What about you, Mog?" said the granny.
But Mog thought the wheels were too surprising.

One day the granny put out her best tea cups.
She said, "We're going to have a party."
It was very hot, so they had the party in the yard.

A lot of other grannies came. They were surprised to see Mog.
The granny told them about Mog's people. She said,
"They've been all over America and now they're ending up
at a special Red Indian show."

The grannies stayed a long time.
Mog got very tired.
She thought of Debbie and
she wondered what Red Indians were.

Suddenly a picture of Debbie came into her head.

Debbie was smiling at a big bird.

Mog knew it was a bird because it had feathers.

But it had a face like a person. It was a person bird.

And there were more person birds nearby.

Why was Debbie smiling? Those big person birds

might fly away with her and hurt her.

Mog wanted to save Debbie.

She did a big jump.

Tibbles liked tea inside him, not outside.

"Oh dear," said the granny.

"Oh dear," said all the other grannies.
"And your best cup too." Then they went home.

That night Mog did not
sleep in the granny's bed.
She was too sad.

She was still sad in the morning.
She thought of Tibbles and
the granny being upset.
She thought of Debbie
and the person birds.

Suddenly a picture of Debbie came into her head.
The person birds had not hurt her at all.
Instead they had given her some of their feathers
and a baby person bird as a present. She was
smiling and excited, and she was coming home.
Mog thought, "I must be there to meet her."

She ran out of the yard

and across a road

and down another road

...and up a tree.

After a time the dog went home.
Mog wanted to go home too,
but she couldn't get down the tree.

She tried this way

and that way,

but she was stuck,
and it was getting late,
and Debbie would
be coming home.

Mog thought, "There's nobody to help me."
But there was somebody.

"Quick, Mog! Jump!" said the granny,
and Mog jumped.

"We'll have to get a move on," said the granny.

"We haven't much time," said the granny.

"I think we can just make it," said the granny.

AND THEY DID!

When Debbie got home, Mog was there to meet her.

"We've never had such excitement," said the granny.
"Mog will have to come and stay with Tibbles again."

Mog said nothing.

She didn't like things to be exciting.

She liked them to be the same.